JESSAME
to the *RESCUE
and other stories

Other books by
JULIA JARMAN

JESSAME
to the RESCUE

and other stories

JULIA JARMAN

Illustrated by Duncan Smith

Andersen Press • London

This edition first published in Great Britain in 2008 by
ANDERSEN PRESS LIMITED
20 Vauxhall Bridge Road
London SW1V 2SA
www.andersenpress.co.uk

First published in 1997 by Mammoth, an imprint of Reed International Books

British Library Cataloguing in Publication Data available.

ISBN 978 184 270 8309

Printed and bound in Great Britain by CPI Bookmarque, Croydon, CR0 4TD

For Joshua with love

Some more stories about your mum when she was a little girl.

Contents

1
A hedgehog day

ONE DAY JESSAME Aduke – say 'A-doo-kay' – Olusanya was playing marbles with her friend Jason. Jason went to the same school as Jessame and he was the caretaker's son, but they were playing at 56 Holly Bush House because that was where Jessame lived. She lived with her mum, her little brother, Mark, and Grandma and Grandpa Williams – and Jacko the parrot. Holly Bush House was a very smart block of flats in Holly Bush Gardens in Bethnal Green, and Jessame and Jason were playing outside on the green verandah. The green verandah stretched from number 58 to number 52. Uncle Sharp lived at number

52; Vicki and Penny lived at number 54 and Mrs Balalaika lived at number 58. Today Mrs Balalaika was having a chinwag with Grandma Williams, and Jessame and Jason were listening as they rolled their marbles.

Jessame liked listening to grown-ups talking, but Grandma didn't like Jessame listening, not secretly. She called it 'sticky-beaking' and she said 'sticky-beaks' would hear no good of themselves, but it wasn't true. Jessame often heard Grandma boasting – about Jessame! That's why she liked listening. In fact, Grandma was boasting now!

'Jessame eats everything,' she was saying to Mrs Balalaika. 'She isn't fussy at all. Whatever I cook, Jessame eats it. She's a joy to cook for. Now Mark, he's different. He eats nothing at all. Except biscuits,' she added, moving a packet of

biscuits out of the way of Mark. He was on the rug playing with bricks. Jessame could see him because the door was open.

'Is it true?' Jason's freckled face looked amazed. 'Do you really eat everything?'

Jessame laughed.

'Do you even eat cabbage?' Jason said. He hated cabbage and he wouldn't eat one little bit.

'Listen,' said Jessame, for Grandma was telling Mrs Balalaika all the things that Jessame would eat.

'Her favourite is chicken with spinach sauce.'

'Yuk,' said Jason. 'Spinach.'

'She likes okra,' said Grandma. 'She loves chicken okra.'

'What's okra?' said Jason.

'Lady's fingers,' said Jessame, spidering her fingers at him – and Jason's freckles went quite pale.

'She eats sweet potato and plantain. She loves plantain chips.'

'Yuk,' said Jason. 'Sweet potatoes. Do you have sugar on them?'

Jessame giggled.

'Go on, tell me. Do you really eat everything?' said Jason.

'Yes!' said Jessame – and Grandma coughed. So did Jacko. Jacko was an African grey parrot who was very good at talking. He had a bright red tail and he lived at Holly Bush House too.

There was a pot of yellow nasturtiums on the verandah.

'Do you eat flowers?' said Jason.

'And leaves and caterpillars,' said Jessame. 'I like them fried.'

Jason laughed, then he looked all around – and he became very silly. 'Do you eat paint?' he said, looking at the bright green railings.

'Yes,' said Jessame and Grandma coughed again and so did Jacko.

'That's a bad cough you've got,' said Mrs Balalaika.

'I think it's the draught from that door,' said Grandma.

But Jessame wasn't listening to Grandma and Mrs Balalaika any more. She was having much too much fun with Jason, who was looking through the railings of the verandah. Number 56 Holly Bush House was on the second floor and you could see the railway below.

'Do you eat soot?' said Jason, because the railway arches were ever so sooty and cobwebby.

'And cobwebs,' said Jessame.

'Do you eat trains?' said Jason as a train went past.

'Yum, yum, yum!' shouted Jessame, and the two of them laughed so much they nearly fell over.

Then Grandma came outside and said, 'I think we should be going now. Put your marbles away, you two, and wash your hands. And make haste now.'

Grandma Williams was taking Jessame and Jason to see Aunt Sybil, who lived at Heathrow, near the airport. They were going on the train. Jason was going with them because he liked aeroplanes.

'Goodbye. See you soon,' said Jacko when he saw everyone getting ready.

'Goodbye. See you soon,' said Jessame. 'Wish me luck, Jacko.'

She said 'Wish me luck,' because she didn't much like the journey to Aunt Sybil's. She didn't like travelling on the Underground. So she was glad Jason was there to take her mind off it.

Jason carried on playing the Do You Eat? game:

'Do you eat tickets?' he said as they stood at the ticket office at Bethnal Green Station waiting for Grandma to buy the tickets, and Jessame giggled. 'Do you eat baby-buggies? Do you eat babies?'

Jessame giggled again, and Baby Mark who was in the buggy giggled too. Jessame even giggled when they started going downstairs to the Underground, but she stopped when they reached the platform. For there was a dark, dark, tunnel staring at them, and she had to remind herself that a train was going to come out of the tunnel – and not a monster, and that was hard because the train sounded like a monster and it looked like a monster.

First you heard a rumbling.

Then you saw two big eyes coming out of the darkness!

Then you heard a roaring and the two big eyes came closer!

'Do you eat umbrellas?' said Jason, pointing to a man with an umbrella – he had it up in the underground – and Jessame laughed so much she didn't notice the train stopping in front of her. There it was, a nice silvery train with its doors sliding open.

'Do you eat doors?' said Jason as the doors closed.

'Do you eat maps?' he said as they sat down and stared at the map on the wall.

Jessame giggled but Grandma Williams sighed very hard. Jessame thought Grandma was fed up with the Do You Eat? game. But Jason kept on.

'Do you eat darkness?' he said as it went very dark.

'Do you eat hats?' he said as it became light again and they arrived at Holborn Station where they had to change trains. A man wearing a hat with ear flaps got on.

'Do you eat ear flaps?' said Jason.

Jessame laughed so much she nearly didn't get off the train in time.

When they were on the next train, Grandma took some peanut butter sandwiches out of her bag and they had four each.

Suddenly it was very light as the underground train turned into an above-the-ground train and they could see grass and trees and cows!

'Do you eat cows?' said Jason.

'Of course!' said Jessame and she fell off her seat with laughing.

Grandma said, 'That's enough of that game. We're nearly there. Why don't you look out of the window for aeroplanes?'

They saw a Jumbo jet and a Boeing 757 and an airbus. Then they were at Hounslow Station and Grandma Williams said, 'I want a promise from you two. No more of that silly game, please.'

Jessame and Jason promised and then they saw Aunt Sybil's son, Garfield, running to meet them. First he swung Jessame into the air and then he swung Jason.

Garfield said he went to circus school on Saturdays. He knew how to juggle and how to walk on stilts and he would show them later. He said he was really pleased to see them. He told them his mum had bought lots of nice things to eat that she didn't usually buy.

It was quite a walk to Aunt Sybil's house, but Garfield carried their bags. When they got there, Aunt Sybil rushed out to hug and kiss them all, even Jason – which took him by surprise. She said lunch wasn't quite ready, but if they were hungry they could have a chocolate biscuit each and a drink of ice-cream soda.

Afterwards, Aunt Sybil took them to see the conservatory. It was a little glass house on the end of the brick house and there were lots of plants in it. It looked like a little jungle and it was very hot. They all said how very nice it was and Jessame said she wished she'd brought Jacko, because he'd have liked it. He really would.

Jessame and Jason went into the

garden with Garfield and he juggled with three balls, and then with five. Jessame and Jason had a go – with two balls – and after that Garfield showed them how to walk on stilts.

Suddenly there was a scream.

It came from the conservatory.

They all ran to see – even Garfield who was on stilts.

Aunt Sybil was standing on a chair and Grandma was saying, 'Don't be silly, Sybil. They won't hurt you.'

'What won't hurt her?' said Jessame.

'Hedgehogs,' said Grandma. 'But be very quiet or they'll go away. Look.'

There was a family of hedgehogs on the floor of the conservatory, a mother and three babies. Jessame had never seen a real hedgehog before and nor had Jason, so they kept very, very quiet while Grandma got the hedgehogs a saucer of milk. The three of them knelt down to look at them as the prickly mother hedgehog started to drink.

'Sluff, sluff, sluff.' She drank the milk noisily, but the baby hedgehogs were too little to reach the saucer. They had soft pink noses and they looked knobbly. Their prickles hadn't grown yet. Jessame

felt sorry for them, but the mother hedgehog did a very clever thing. She put out a paw and tipped up the saucer so milk spilled on to the floor.

Aunt Sybil started to tut about the mess, but everybody shushed her as the baby hedgehogs started to drink.

'Sluff, sluff, sluff.' Soon the puddle had gone! Then the mother hedgehog started to scurry towards the door, and the baby hedgehogs followed her.

'Well,' said Aunt Sybil, 'looking at hedgehogs won't get the dinner ready. And I haven't even thought of a pudding yet. Come on, Garfield, you must help.'

Grandma went into the house too, but Jessame and Jason followed the hedgehogs who were heading for the leafy hedge at the back of the flower border. They watched them until they had tunnelled under a pile of leaves and out of sight.

'What shall we do now?' said Jason.

Garfield had taken his juggling things and his stilts into the house.

'We could look at planes,' said Jessame, but the sky was empty. 'We could look at flowers,' she added.

'No, they're boring,' said Jason. His eyes were gleaming, so Jessame wasn't a bit surprised when he said, 'Do you eat hedgehogs, Jessame?'

'YES!' she said. 'YES! YES! YES!' She laughed and laughed until she heard a cough, and there was Grandma Williams standing right by her. Had she heard?

She didn't say anything about fibs or promises. She just said she'd thought what she could do for pudding and she'd send Garfield when dinner was ready.

Jessame found a bit of paper and a pencil in her pocket and she played noughts and crosses with Jason. When he said, 'Do you eat pencils, Jessame? Do you eat paper?' she didn't answer him. She really didn't. But noughts and crosses wasn't as good as the Do You Eat? game and it seemed ages before Garfield came out to say dinner was ready.

The dinner on the table looked delicious. It was chicken and rice, and Aunt Sybil gave her a big plateful. Grandma said, 'Leave some room for the next course, Jessame.'

Jessame said, 'What's the next course?'

And Grandma said, 'Hedgehog.'

'Hedgehog! Not the one . . .'

She looked to see if Grandma was joking, but Grandma looked very serious. She said, 'Not the one we've just been looking at, Jessame. Of course not. I've cooked another one.'

Then Jessame remembered how Grandma didn't like fibs and she didn't like broken promises. She said, 'I don't think I'll have room for pudding. This chicken and rice is so delicious.'

But Grandma said, 'Oh, you must have some hedgehog, Jessame. I baked it specially.'

Baked hedgehog! Jessame had read a book once about long ago when people baked hedgehogs. She didn't know what to say.

Jason was silent. Jessame could feel him being silent. He was waiting – to see if she would eat the hedgehog.

Jessame thought, this really isn't fair. Grandma started it when she said, 'Jessame eats everything.'

Aunt Sybil said, 'Eat up, everyone, before it goes cold.'

Everyone ate up, though Jessame's

plate wasn't quite as clean as it usually was.

Then Aunt Sybil cleared the dishes and Grandma said, 'I'll go and get the hedgehog.'

Now Jason's eyes said, *Do you eat hedgehogs, Jessame?* And Jessame thought, I'm going to have to eat it.

And then Grandma came in grandly holding a dish above her head with one hand.

She lowered it on to the table – and there it was – the hedgehog.

Its body was made of cake covered with thick chocolate icing.

Its prickles were made of almonds.

Its pink nose was a jelly sweet.

Its beady eyes were liquorice.

At first Jessame didn't want to eat it, because it looked too good to eat.

'But you've got to eat it,' Jason said.

'You said you eat anything, Jessame.' So of course she did – and so did Jason. Everybody had a piece and it was delicious. The chocolate icing was soft yet stiff and very sweet, and the cake was buttery and yellow and springy.

There was some left over. Aunt Sybil put it in a bag for Jessame and Jason to eat on the train journey home. Jessame saved hers and when she got home she gave the cake to Grandpa who said, 'What sort of day have you had, Jessame Aduke?' Grandpa always called her Jessame Aduke.

And she said, 'I've had a hedgehog day, Grandpa, thank you very much. I've had a very hedgehog day.'

Then Grandpa shared his piece of cake with Jessame.

2
The Ship of Fancy

Jessame liked Saturdays, because she always did something interesting with Grandpa. Sometimes they went to the museum and sometimes they went to the library, which were both in Cambridge Heath Road. Sometimes they went to the museum *and* the library.

If it was fine they went to Victoria Park. Victoria Park was fun. There was miles and miles of grass and lots of birds and animals. There were three white geese who marched in step as if they were in the army, and there were dozens of rabbits and guinea pigs. One of the rabbits, which was bigger than the others and black all over, knew Jessame.

Jessame called him Brer Rabbit after the rabbit in her favourite stories – and when she called him he came right up to her and whiffled his pink nose! He was clever just like the rabbit in the story.

So Jessame liked going to Victoria Park and she liked going home again afterwards, because they always called in at the Galleon Café. There was a pretty picture on the wall. It was of a galleon which was a ship with many sails, and the picture was embroidered. If you sat at the table just below the picture you could see all the tiny stitches, and the tiny stitches of the words underneath the red and gold galleon with its puffy white sails. The words said:

A Ship is a Breath of Romance
That carries us miles away.
But stories are ships of Fancy
That can sail on any day.

Jessame loved stories. That's why she went to the library almost every Saturday. She loved books because they were full of stories, and she loved Grandpa because he was full of stories too! Grandpa had been a sailor and he knew stories from all over the world. Sometimes when Grandpa told her a story about India or America or Africa – she felt as if she had sailed away to a far-away country.

She knew exactly what the words under the picture meant. Fancy – it was a lovely word. Jessame liked saying it. 'Fancy this' and 'fancy that' and 'fancy dress' and Grandma called little cakes with icing on them 'fancies'.

Grandpa said fancy meant 'imagine', and Jessame and Grandpa imagined ever such a lot. They imagined that the petrol pump on the way to Victoria Park was an alien from outer space.

The petrol pump stood all by itself outside a garage on Old Ford Road. The garage man served you himself from the petrol pump which was bright pink with black arms. Well, the pipes looked like black arms and the petrol gauge looked like an alien's head, and once Grandpa stood behind the petrol pump and said, 'Take me to your leader!' in a Daleky sort of voice. Jessame pretended she was the leader and Grandpa was the alien from outer space. She took him by the hand and led him to Victoria Park and showed him all the things there. Grandpa pretended he hadn't seen any of them before, and she had to explain what they were very carefully, or he'd do silly things like try to eat the grass!

Yes, Saturdays were good fun. There was so much that Jessame and Grandpa could do on Saturdays that they spent all Friday evening deciding.

One Friday they decided to do something extra specially interesting, something really different. They decided to go and see a real old sailing ship, a galleon, just like the one in the picture. It was called the *Cutty Sark*. You can imagine how Jessame felt about that.

And you can imagine how she felt when she woke up on that particular Saturday morning and she didn't feel very well.

At first she thought she was just tired because she'd found it ever so hard to get to sleep the night before. But then she felt very hot and sticky and very cold and shivery all at the same time, and then she sneezed, and Mum came into her bedroom. She felt Jessame's forehead and said, 'I think you'd better stay there this morning, Jessame. You've got a bit of a temperature.'

'No, no,' Jessame wailed, 'I want to get up!' though she didn't really feel like getting up.

Mark, Jessame's little brother who was just learning to speak said, 'Stay there!' as if she were a dog!

Mum came back with a thermometer. She took Jessame's temperature and said it was 38°C, so she had to stay in bed.

Grandma brought her breakfast in bed. It was on a tea-tray covered with a

lace cloth and Grandpa said, 'Aren't you going to look under the cloth, Jessame Aduke? It's not every day you get breakfast in bed.'

But Jessame didn't feel like looking. She was so disappointed.

Grandpa said, 'You wouldn't enjoy a boat trip feeling under the weather, Jessame Aduke. And just look at that rain! We couldn't have gone anywhere.'

Jessame knew he was right, but she didn't feel like saying so. She stuck out her bottom lip. She couldn't help it.

Grandpa continued: 'All I can offer is the Ship of Fancy today, Jessame. We can sail away on that if you like?'

Well, Jessame couldn't be grumpy with Grandpa for long. 'Can Jacko come too, Grandpa?' she asked.

'I'll call him,' said Grandpa. He did and the parrot came flying through the door and landed on Jessame's bed. First he pecked her ear several times, very gently – it was his way of kissing – then he perched on the rocking-chair beside her bed, where Grandpa was sitting.

'Where would you like to go?' said Grandpa.

'Africa,' said Jessame. 'Jacko would like to go to Africa.' That's where Jacko had come from. He was an African grey parrot, with a splendid red tail.

'Africa,' said Jacko.

'And who would you like to meet there?' said Grandpa.

'Brer Rabbit of course,' said Jessame.

'Rabbit,' said Jacko.

'OK,' said Grandpa, leaning back and closing his eyes. 'Now, have I ever told you the one about Brer Rabbit and the big fierce tiger?'

'But there aren't any tigers in Africa!'

said Jessame. 'You've told me that lots of times.'

'But have I ever told you why not?' said Grandpa.

'No,' said Jessame.

'Then listen,' said Grandpa, closing his eyes again. 'Once upon a time in Africa there was a big fierce tiger, a she-tiger, ten feet long from the tip of her nose to the end of her tail. That's nearly as long as your room, Jessame Aduke. She was a fierce and powerful cat and all the other animals were afraid of her.'

'Even Brer Rabbit, Grandpa?'

'Even Brer Rabbit.' Grandpa went on: 'Now, one day Tiger was walking through the forest when she saw Brer Rabbit.

'"Brer Rabbit, what are you doing?" said Tiger, rather surprised that the rabbit hadn't run away like all the other animals. Indeed, Brer Rabbit would have run away if he had seen Tiger coming, but he'd been too busy eating. Now he had to think very quickly – so he began to pull vines from off the trees.

'"Oh, Tiger, don't you know, there's a storm coming? I'm going to tie myself to a tree in a minute, with these long vines, so that the storm doesn't blow me away. When the storm comes anyone who isn't tied to a tree will be blown away."

'"Will they?" said Tiger.

'"Oh, yes," said Brer Rabbit, pulling down vines very quickly.

'Tiger looked worried. Very worried. She looked at the vines and wondered how she could tie herself to a tree. Then she said, in a wheedling sort of voice, "Brer Rabbit, could you tie me to a tree too, please, so that I don't blow away?"

'Brer Rabbit carried on pulling down

vines very, very quickly. "Sorry, Tiger, the storm will be here soon. I must tie myself and you must tie yourself, I'm afraid."

'But Tiger knew she couldn't tie herself tightly. "Brer Rabbit," she said, "you're so clever. You're much much better at tying than me. Please, please, tie me to a tree."

'So Brer Rabbit wound the vines round and round till Tiger was bound tight to the tree. Then he ran off – with a skip and a bounce – because there was no storm coming. It was all a trick to escape from Tiger.

'You can imagine how Tiger felt. First she waited for the storm to come – and it never did. Then she tried to untie the vines, but she couldn't. She cried for help but none of the other animals would help her.

'"If we untie you you'll eat us," they said.

'By this time Tiger was very, very angry. She stayed angry till Vulture came along. Vulture helped Tiger, but only after she'd promised to share all her killings with him. That's why Tiger never eats all she kills but always leaves a little something for Vulture.

'Tiger was still very angry with Brer Rabbit. She was determined to kill him. Day after day she roamed the forest looking for him. And one day she came up behind him – on the top of a rock, gazing into a forest pool.

'"Brer Rabbit, I am going to eat you," said Tiger.

'Brer Rabbit froze. He hadn't heard Tiger approach and he was afraid, but he thought very quickly.

'"Oh, d-don't eat me yet," he said.

"Do look at this first."

'"What?" said Tiger.

'"Look," said Brer Rabbit, "Look down there at that beautiful golden ball."

'Tiger stepped forward. "What golden ball?" he said.

'Brer Rabbit pointed to the reflection of the sun in the pool below. It gleamed and glittered and filled the pool with brightness.

'"Ah, if only we could get that golden ball out," said Brer Rabbit. "We'd be richer than the king if we had that."

'"I could get it out," said Tiger. "For both of us," she added quickly, though she really intended to grab the ball and run away with it. "You're too small to carry it, but I could get it out."

'"Could
you?" said
Brer
Rabbit. "That
would be nice, but
when you get hold of it,
don't let it slip or it will
go deeper and deeper."

'Quickly Tiger dived in, but
she came up spluttering, without
the ball.

'Brer Rabbit called out:

"Tiger, my friend, be brave, be bold.
Go deeper and deeper to find the gold."

'Tiger dived in again, but she came up
again without the golden ball. She was
spluttering and gasping, but Brer Rabbit
urged her to have another go.

37

"Tiger, my friend, be brave and bold.
Go deeper still to find the gold!"

'This time Tiger dived so deep that she never came up again. She dived so deep that she came out on the other side of the ocean in India, where she lives to this day. That's why there are no tigers in Africa, Jessame Aduke,' said Grandpa.

'I'd like to go to Africa,' said Jessame, 'and India.'

'You will,' said Grandpa, 'some day, and even sooner than that you'll be sailing up the Thames to Greenwich.'

'Sailing! But you said the *Cutty Sark* wasn't in the water, Grandpa!'

'She isn't, Jessame Aduke, but the *Eleanor Rose* and the *Sarah Kathleen* and *Rosewood* are in the water. They're river launches and you'll be on one of them

38

next Saturday if the weather is fine. Now, aren't you going to eat a little breakfast? See what your Grandma has made you.'

Then Jessame lifted the lacy cloth and saw the dainty sandwiches – shaped like all her favourite things.

'Ships!' she cried. 'And rabbits and parrots – oh, sorry Jacko!'

She started to eat them, but Jacko didn't stay to watch. He flew back into the kitchen.

3

All aboard the *Eleanor Rose*!

It was Saturday morning again – at last! Jessame and Grandpa were standing on the green verandah of Holly Bush House, but Grandpa looked grave.

'Look at that sky, Jessame Aduke.' Grandpa pointed to the clouds. They were only little clouds but there were lots of them – in rows, so that the sky looked scaly like a fish. 'It's a mackerel sky. You know what that means.'

'Mackerel sky, mackerel sky, not long wet, not long dry,' chanted Jessame, who knew all Grandpa's old sea-sayings. 'But we are going, Grandpa, even if it does rain. We're having a picnic in Victoria

Park, then we're going to see the *Cutty Sark*. That rhymes!'

Jessame was all ready to go. She had her mac and her umbrella and the camera Grandma and Grandpa had given her for her birthday, and the little straw basket Aunt Gbee had brought all the way from Africa. She was going to carry her picnic in that. Grandma Williams was in the kitchen making the picnic right now.

'I think it might be better to leave your basket behind, Jessame Aduke. Grandma can put your picnic in her bag with everyone else's,' said Grandpa.

But Jessame was determined to take her own little basket. She would put her picnic in it and her camera.

She hurried to the kitchen to see what they were going to eat, and as she ran she sang, 'We're having a picnic in Victoria Park. And

we're going to see the *Cutty Sark*!'

'Not Victoria Park, Jessame. That's in Bethnal Green,' said Grandma, who had made two sorts of sandwiches and three sorts of cake. 'We're going to have the picnic in Victoria Tower Gardens. It's by the river next to the Houses of Parliament. It's quite a journey, so we'd better make haste.'

Grandma was right It was a long bus journey to Victoria Tower Gardens and as they arrived Big Ben was booming! He was much bigger and much louder than Jessame thought he'd be. He struck twelve as Grandma set out the picnic on a red and white tablecloth.

There were corned beef sandwiches which were Jessame's favourite at the moment, and ham sandwiches with pepper sauce, which were Grandpa's favourite of all time. There was lots of fruit and crème caramels in little pots. Crème caramel is a delicious custard with bitter-sweet toffee on top – and Jessame loved it. There was apricot and orange juice and the three sorts of cake – banana cake, coconut cake and sugar cake which had a crunchy layer of brown sugar on top – and coffee for the grown-ups out of Grandpa's flask.

Jessame was a bit worried when a policeman stopped to talk to them, though she couldn't see a KEEP OFF THE GRASS sign anywhere, but the policeman was very friendly. He had a round, smiley face and said, 'That looks like a very nice picnic.'

Mark offered him a sandwich. He really did. He held out a corned beef sandwich – with only one bite out of it – and said, 'Nice. Policeman have.'

The policeman said, 'Thank you, but no thank you.' He wasn't allowed to eat on duty, he said. Then he asked Mark what his name was, and he asked Jessame what her name was. Then Jessame asked the policeman what his name was and he said, 'Roman.'

'Well, I've heard of Roman soldiers, but I didn't know there were Roman policemen,' said Grandpa.

Jessame laughed. So did the policeman. He said Roman was his Christian name and it was Polish. His surname was Kulakov and that was

Ukrainian. His mum came from Poland and his dad came from the Ukraine. Jessame started to tell him that Grandpa came from Africa and Grandma came from the West Indies, but Big Ben boomed again.

'Goodness gracious me,' said Grandma, 'one o'clock already. We should be on the boat by now. Make haste everyone!'

Everybody helped pack up very quickly, then they ran out of the gardens, past the Houses of Parliament and into a tunnel which went under the Houses of Parliament to Westminster Pier. Mark was lucky. He was in the buggy and Grandma pushed him, but Jessame had to run all the way holding Grandpa's hand.

Luckily they were just in time. The big wide boat was just about to leave. 'All aboard the *Eleanor Rose*!' shouted the

captain as they ran up the gangplank.
Then the boat started up.

When Jessame got her breath back, she
began to feel very excited about riding in
a boat. She had a seat near the side and
she could see the sun on the River
Thames below, and Big Ben looking
down on them. The red and gold
decorations round his face glittered.

'We're lucky with the weather,' said
Jessame's mum.

'So far,' said Grandpa.

'God bless the sunlight,' said
Grandma.

Then the boat rumbled and roared –
because it was a launch with a diesel
engine not a sailing boat – and they were
on their way!

The front of the boat – Grandpa called it the bow – swung round as the captain in the wheelhouse turned a big wooden wheel. Then it swung even further round so that they were facing the sea, though they weren't going all the way to the sea. They were going as far as Greenwich and it would take nearly an hour.

They went under Charing Cross Bridge, which was a railway bridge. A train was going over it, so that was lucky. Then Grandpa took Jessame to the back of the boat, which he called the stern, so that she could see the wake. That was the V-shaped track the boat made in the water. It was a nice feeling watching the wake getting wider and wider behind them – and it was nice having Grandpa to point out all the sights.

There was Cleopatra's Needle, which wasn't a needle but a tall column brought from Ancient Egypt. There was St Paul's Cathedral with its big round dome. There was Sir Christopher Wren's little house on the other side of the river nearly opposite, and they went under eight bridges, all different. Jessame liked Tower Bridge best because it was blue and gold and it opened and closed – though it didn't when the *Eleanor Rose* went under because she wasn't tall. And on the left hand bank, beside Tower Bridge, there was the Tower of London, which wasn't just a tower, it was a whole castle. Grandpa said the crown jewels were kept there, guarded by Beefeaters.

Suddenly Jessame said, 'I want to take a photograph of that!'

Grandpa said, 'Where's your camera then?'

'It's at the bottom of my little basket,' she said, then realised her basket wasn't over her arm. 'Where is my basket?' she wailed.

'When did you have it last, Jessame Aduke?' Grandpa asked.

'When we were having our picnic,' said Jessame.

'Oh dear,' they both said.

Losing her little basket and her camera didn't completely spoil Jessame's day but it did make her sad. Grandpa said they would go and look for it when they got back to Westminster Pier, and he said she must hope. It might still be in Victoria Tower Gardens, lying on the grass.

Just then it started to rain, so they all went downstairs to the lounge. They spent the rest of the voyage looking at the rain trickling down the window panes. But when they left the boat at Greenwich, it stopped raining and the sun came out!

Nothing could stop Jessame enjoying the *Cutty Sark*. It was like the ship in the Galleon Café, but even more beautiful. Jessame loved its wavy, in-and-out shape. She loved its ever-so-tall masts. She loved the patterns of the masts and the rigging against the sky.

Grandpa said the *Cutty Sark* wasn't just beautiful, she'd been useful too. She was a clipper and she used to bring tea all the way from China. The wind once carried her a thousand miles in three days. A thousand miles! Grandma said she really was a Breath of Romance.

'She?' said Jessame. Grandpa said that boats are always 'she'.

Jessame said she was graceful – like a dancer – a dancer standing on tiptoe, because that's what she looked like balancing on her pointed keel.

Grandpa said she was over a hundred

years old, but she looked shiny and new. She was painted black and decorated with white and gold patterns and writing. There was a cat's head on one side – made of gold! – and a beautiful lady in a white dress was hanging over the bows. Grandpa said she was the ship's figure-head, though she was a whole lady not just a head. He said her name was Nannie, and she was Scottish and her white dress was called a cutty sark. That's why the ship was called the *Cutty Sark*.

'*Cutty Sark*.' Jessame liked saying it.

She wanted to go inside, but Mark wanted to feed the pigeons and seagulls – so Jessame went in with Grandpa. First they went into the hold at the bottom where all the cargo was kept. That was quite dark. Then they climbed some stairs to the top deck and, with his camera, Grandpa took a photo of Jessame, her hands on the big ship's wheel.

Jessame said, 'I'd like to be a sailor.'

'Come and see where you'd have to live, then,' said Grandpa.

The cabins were on the top deck. You went down some steps to the captain's cabin. It was cosy like a little sitting-room. It even had a fireplace. The captain had his own kitchen and a bathroom, and everything in it looked comfortable and shiny. But the ordinary sailors' quarters weren't cosy at all. They had narrow little bunks to sleep on and their kitchen was much smaller than the captain's, though twenty-eight of them had to share it.

'Poor things,' said Jessame.

'If you do go to sea, Jessame, make sure you're the captain!' said Grandpa.

Before they left he bought Jessame and Mark captains' hats from the souvenir shop. They needed them on the journey back because it started to rain again.

'Look out for a rainbow,' said Grandma, when the sun came out.

'Why?' asked Jessame.

'Because you can wish,' said Grandma.

'And you often see rainbows when there's sun and rain together,' Grandpa explained. 'Rainbows are all the colours of the sun reflected in raindrops. Red, orange, yellow, green, blue, indigo and violet – in that order.'

'How do you know?' said Jessame.

'Richard of York gave battle in vain,' said Grandpa. Jessame was just going to ask what he meant when she saw an arch of red and orange in the steely grey sky, then yellow and green and blue and dark blue and purple!

'A rainbow!' cried Jessame.

'Where?' said Mark, then he saw it too, a very pale rainbow. It began on the South Bank behind the old County Hall and it ended behind the Houses of Parliament. But as they watched, the colours grew brighter and brighter and Jessame closed her eyes and wished.

Can you guess what she wished for? Well, a few moments later, when they were at the top of the gangplank saying goodbye to the captain of the *Eleanor Rose*, Mark said, 'Policeman. Nice Policeman,' and there was PC Roman Kulakov, standing at the end of the gangway, and do you know what he had in his hand? He had Jessame's little basket, and her camera was at the bottom!

4

The new girl

Grandpa could speak seven languages! He could speak English, because he'd learned English at school when he was a boy in Africa, and he'd spoken Croo and Creole at home. Then he learned Portuguese and Greek and Spanish and French when he became a sailor. Grandpa was a telephone engineer now, but when he'd been a sailor he'd sailed right round the world.

Jessame thought Grandpa was very clever to be able to speak so many languages, but Grandpa said it wasn't many really. He told Jessame that in the whole wide world there are over ten thousand languages. There are a thousand languages just in Africa and twenty-two of them in Sierra Leone where Grandpa came from.

Jessame loved to hear Grandpa speak in different languages. And she loved speaking in different languages – and she could, just a bit, because Grandpa had taught her. Grandpa was very good at teaching. He taught Jessame how to say hello in five languages and a few other words as well, so she thought she might be able to help with the new girl.

The new girl was in Jessame's class at St John's Primary School and she was very quiet. Mrs Pearce, Jessame's teacher, said her name was Tembi. She came from North Africa, but Mrs Pearce didn't know which part of North Africa, because Tembi didn't answer when Mrs Pearce spoke to her.

So Jessame asked her. First she just smiled to be friendly, but Tembi couldn't see that Jessame was smiling and friendly because she was sitting at a table with her head in her hands. Jessame tapped her very gently on the shoulder – but Tembi didn't look up. Jessame said 'nafwawa', which means hello in Croo and 'holay', which means hello in Creole, but Tembi still didn't answer.

So Jessame said, 'Na usi you from?' which is 'Where do you come from?' in Creole.

But Tembi sat as if she hadn't heard Jessame.

She sat as if she didn't hear anybody, though she did get up when everybody else got up to go into the hall for PE.

When Mrs Pearce said everybody had to get a partner, Jessame went up to Tembi, who was standing at the side of

the hall looking at her feet. But she carried on looking at her feet, even when Jessame held out her hands and said, 'Would you like to be my partner?' She said it in English because she didn't know how to say that in any other language. Tembi just stood, so Jessame had to be Jason's partner.

At playtime Jessame and Jamila and Gemma went up to Tembi. They held out their hands and they pointed out of the window, to show her that they wanted her to come out to play. It was a very nice spring day and there were interesting things to do in the playground, but Tembi just sat at her table. So she didn't see the slide or the playbars or the climbing frame.

Mrs Pearce said she thought Tembi was overwhelmed, but Jessame said she thought she was sad.

That night she told Grandpa about her.

He said, 'I expect she's feeling like a fish out of water, Jessame. It'll take her a few days to get used to things. You just carry on being kind though. I'm sure she notices that even if she doesn't seem to.'

It was hard being kind to Tembi. Next day at school Jessame watched her arrive. She arrived with two tall people.

Jessame thought they must be her mum and dad. They wore African clothes and they looked a bit sad too as they helped Tembi take off her coat, but when Jessame smiled at them, they smiled back. Tembi didn't smile.

Jessame waved goodbye, and they waved goodbye, but Tembi didn't. She didn't wave goodbye to her own mum and dad! So Jessame went up to Tembi when they'd gone and put her arm round her, and Tembi shouted! She shouted loudly as if Jessame had hurt her. And everybody looked at Jessame as if Jessame *had* hurt her.

Tony Lumsley said, 'Leave her alone!'

Mrs Pearce came up, but she didn't blame Jessame. She said, 'I'd leave Tembi on her own if I were you, till she gets used to us.'

Jessame wondered when that would

be.

That night, when they were all talking on the green verandah, Grandpa said, 'How was Tembi today?'

'She was cross,' said Jessame.

She told Grandpa how Tembi had shouted at her.

Grandma said, 'She sounds as if she's full of sadness.'

Jessame said, 'I think she's full of madness.'

Grandpa said, 'Give her time. Be patient, Jessame Aduke.'

But Jessame was a bit nervous when she went to school next day. What if Tembi shouted again?

Tembi was sitting in the book corner. She was looking at a book about a rabbit.

It was quite an old book about an old toy rabbit who had come to life when a little boy loved it. Jessame knew the story because Grandpa had read it to her. It was called *The Velveteen Rabbit.*

Jessame thought about Tembi and the book and she had an idea. So she went to tell Mrs Pearce who said, 'Yes. You can try, Jessame.'

Then Jessame found Jason and they both went to see Jason's dad who was the caretaker and, after lunch, Jason's dad came into the classroom with Benjy who was Jason's big, black and white, spotty rabbit.

Mrs Pearce said, 'Quiet please, everyone. Mr Bennet has brought Jason's rabbit in. His name is Benjy.'

Then Mr Bennet took Benjy to the front of the class, and Jason lifted him out of the box. Benjy was very tame. He didn't mind being lifted. He looked all around and he whiffled his nose. Then Jason put him on Mrs Pearce's table with

a carrot to eat and everyone was so quiet you could hear Benjy crunching.

Jessame looked at Benjy, but mostly she looked at Tembi – and Tembi was looking.

She was still in the book corner, still holding the same book, but she was looking at Benjy.

When Mrs Pearce said, 'Put up your hand if you'd like to stroke Benjy very gently,' nearly everyone put up a hand except Tembi, and she didn't come out when the others came out to have their turn at stroking.

Afterwards everyone drew Benjy and some people painted pictures of him. Even Tembi did a drawing. Jessame went to look at it. She thought it was very good, but it wasn't Benjy. Lots of people's rabbit paintings didn't look like Benjy, but Tembi's rabbit was different.

It was more like a toy rabbit than a real rabbit – and it made Jessame wonder.

Perhaps Tembi used to have a toy rabbit that she loved very much, and perhaps she had lost it.

Now, Jessame had Raggy. Raggy had been a ragdoll when Jessame was a baby. She didn't play with her any more, but she still loved Raggy, and when she needed her and couldn't find her it hurt.

Sometimes she couldn't get to sleep without Raggy.

She hated it when her mum washed Raggy.

Perhaps Tembi missed her toy rabbit like that.

Perhaps she'd had to leave it behind when she came to England.

Perhaps she couldn't sleep at night without it. She must be ever so tired. So that's why she just sat. Poor Tembi.

Jessame had an idea. She had an old rabbit somewhere. Grandma had made it for her. Perhaps Grandma would help her make it look like the Velveteen Rabbit. She was very good at making things. She was making toys for the Mission Christmas Bazaar.

But when Grandma came to meet her from school, and Jessame showed her *The Velveteen Rabbit* book she said, 'I don't know, Jessame. I usually have a pattern.'

Jessame said, 'I don't want a new rabbit, Grandma. I want you to help me make my old rabbit look like the Velveteen Rabbit and feel like the Velveteen Rabbit.' She wanted to say – and smell like Tembi's old rabbit, but she didn't see how Grandma could do that.

Grandma said, 'That's a tall order, Jessame. If I remember rightly I made your old rabbit out of corduroy.' Grandma had made Jessame's rabbit from a pair of Grandpa's old trousers.

Jessame found her old rabbit at the bottom of the wardrobe, under some shoes and some fallen-down clothes.

He was dusty and she felt a bit sorry for him. She gave him a cuddle and for a few minutes she wondered if she really wanted to give him to Tembi, and then she decided she did.

She wanted to make Tembi happy.

Grandma wanted to wash him but Jessame said no because he smelled old and brown – and she didn't want the old and brown smell washed away. But she did ask Grandma to mend him because he was torn in places. Grandma mended his nose and mouth with pink stitches and she darned the very thin bits of corduroy. Darning is like weaving.

Jessame took the rabbit to school the very next day. Grandma came too, and they arrived at the same time as Tembi and the tall man and lady. Grandma started talking to them while Jessame and Tembi took their coats off. Tembi went to sit down and Jessame followed her. She put the rabbit on the table in front of her.

Then she waited.

She went to her seat and waited – she didn't just stand and stare – and she saw Tembi look at the brown rabbit. She saw her put out a finger and stroke it. She stroked its back, then she stroked its ears, then she picked it up and she held it against her nose. And suddenly she glanced towards the door where her mum and dad were still talking to Jessame's grandma. She rushed over to them and flung herself at her mum's legs. She was crying, and Jessame was worried – but Grandma came over and told Jessame not to worry. She thought everything was going to be all right.

Jessame said, 'I think I've made her sadder.'

Grandma said, 'I don't think so. She's just letting the sadness out. Look now.'

Jessame saw that Tembi had stopped crying. And she was still holding the brown rabbit – against her nose!

Tembi's dad came over and he said thank you to Jessame. Jessame had guessed right. Tembi had had to leave all her toys behind when they'd come to England in a rush and even her mum and dad hadn't realised how much she'd missed her rabbit. She'd been too sad to tell them.

Tembi and her mum came over and

Tembi gave Jessame a watery smile – and it made her face look lovely!

Then Grandma invited Mr and Mrs Abida – that was their name – and Tembi to tea on Sunday.

'Don't forget to bring Brown Rabbit!' said Jessame.

5

Jessame to the rescue!

Jessame quite liked swimming. She went to swimming class once a week at the York Hall Swimming Baths in Old Ford Road, but she didn't like getting her face wet. So she didn't like jumping in. She didn't mind sliding in, though. It was shivery when the cold water crept over your tummy and up to your armpits, but it was better than plunging.

That's what the teacher, Mrs Crunkle, called jumping in. Mrs Crunkle had lots of chins which covered her neck in folds of skin, like the folds in Uncle Sharp's squeeze box. Jessame thought they were the crunkles. She liked the word crunkle,

73

but she didn't know whether she liked Mrs Crunkle or not. She was quite nice but she did go on about plunging.

At the beginning of the lesson she made everyone line up on the edge of the pool. Then she shouted, 'Come on everybody! Plunge!'

And everybody did, except Jessame.

Mrs Crunkle laughed. She let Jessame slide in and the lesson began. But then Mrs Crunkle told them all to plunge their faces in the water when they were doing the breast-stroke.

Jessame wanted to give up swimming lessons, but her mum said, 'You wanted lessons, Jessame, and I've paid for them. I've paid for ten lessons and you've only had two.'

Grandma and Grandpa Williams agreed with her.

Grandma said, 'It's very important to

learn how to swim. What if you fell in the river, Jessame?'

And Grandpa said, 'You want to learn everything you can, Jessame Aduke.'

So Jessame said, 'Couldn't you teach me how to swim, Grandpa?' Grandpa was very good at teaching and he'd taught Jessame lots of things.

He'd taught her how to do a number eight properly. He said, 'Start at the top and do an S first, then join the ends together.' And it worked!

Grandpa had taught her how to dance in time to music – he'd taught her the waltz, the quickstep and reggae.

Yes, Grandpa was very good at teaching, so Jessame asked him again, 'Please teach me how to swim.'

Grandpa said he would help as long as Jessame kept going to the lessons and really tried.

So she did.

She went to lessons on Tuesday and she went swimming with Grandpa on Sundays – and soon she could swim a whole width. It happened so quickly. One day she couldn't swim because she just couldn't get her foot off the bottom of the pool. Then she could!

It felt like magic!

Being able to swim was wonderful.

Jessame really liked it. But she still didn't like jumping in and she still didn't like putting her face under the water, so she swam with her head stuck up – like a duck! It made Mrs Crunkle sigh and it made Jessame's neck ache, but it was better than getting her nose and eyes full of nasty stinging water.

But one day something happened that changed things.

It was during the summer holidays.

Jessame was on holiday from school and Mark was on holiday from the nursery in Sugar Loaf Lane and Mum was on holiday from the post office where she was secretary to Mr Hankins. It was a very hot day so Jessame's mum said, 'Let's go swimming, shall we? Let's go to the new pool in Barnet.'

Jessame had heard about the new pool. Vicki and Penny from the other end of the green verandah had told her about it. They said it had a fountain and real palm trees and a flume which was a sort of slide-in-a-tunnel – and waves! And it was warm, just like a tropical island.

Jessame was longing to see the waves. Mum said Vicki and Penny could come too if they wanted, so Jessame rushed along the verandah to ask them, and they did want to come and their mum said they could.

Jessame liked Vicki and Penny. They were a bit older than she was and they went to a different school so they didn't play with Jessame very often. Vicki was the eldest and tallest and she had a long fair plait. Penny had bunches usually and freckles always. She had bunches today with butterfly clips.

They went on the bus. It was good going to the pool with Vicki and Penny. They knew where to change into your swimming costume and where to put your clothes, and things like that. So they didn't waste any time.

Jessame put her clothes in a locker of her own and she put the key, which was on a rubber bracelet, round her wrist. Mum put Mark's things in with hers.

Mark was only two and a half, and he hadn't been swimming before. Mum said it was a very good place for his first visit because it was lovely and warm and there was a paddling pool as well as a swimming pool. It was so nice, just like a tropical island. There was even green carpet round the sides of the pool which looked like grass.

Mum said Jessame could go and swim in the swimming pool with Vicki and Penny because they both had certificates for swimming, as long as they didn't go in the deepest water.

Jessame didn't want to go in the deepest water. What if the water went over her head?

Mum stayed with Mark in the paddling pool because she just wanted him to get used to the water, and Jessame stopped with them for a while because Mark was so funny.

Mark wasn't a bit afraid. He splashed a lot. He said he was looking for fishes and

he lay on his tummy saying, 'Mark Shark. Mark Shark,' over and over again.

Jessame pretended to be a fish till Mark bit her ankle. It was only a little bite and it didn't hurt much, but she decided she'd rather play with Vicki and Penny. They were under the fountain in the shallow end of the swimming pool.

Jessame said she hadn't seen any waves yet.

'They start at half past three,' said Vicki, 'and they last for five minutes.'

There was a big clock which nearly filled one wall. It said one minute to half past three!

The waves were great, but Jessame was

glad she was in the shallow end. She could see people in the deep end with waves coming over their faces.

When the waves stopped Vicki and Penny said they wanted to go on the flume. It started very high up and ended in the deep end. You had to climb up lots of steps to get to it and then slide down. Lots of people were going on it. Jessame could see them climbing up. She couldn't see them sliding down because they were in the tunnel, but she could see them coming out and going under the water with a splash. It looked horrible.

She wished she was brave like Vicki and Penny, but she wasn't, so she said she'd go back to her mum and just watch them.

But then the bad things started.

First she couldn't find her mum. She

wasn't in the paddling pool and nor was Mark. Jessame looked and looked but she couldn't see them anywhere.

Then she saw Mark all by himself sitting on the edge of the deep end. He was watching people diving. Jessame didn't yell because she thought the surprise might make him jump and fall in. Or he might turn to look at who was shouting and wobble off the edge. She didn't run for the same reason. Mark looked quite happy watching the divers, and she didn't want to frighten him, so she began to walk towards him quite slowly. He carried on looking at the divers.

Where was her mum? Surely she must be nearby?

But Jessame couldn't see her anywhere.

She carried on walking towards Mark.

She was nearly there with her arms outstretched to pull him away from the edge – when some big children ran by him and he wasn't there any more.

He had fallen in!

Jessame rushed to the edge and saw him at the bottom of the pool.

Now, Mrs Crunkle and Grandpa and everyone had told Jessame lots of times that if you go to the bottom you always bob up again – three times. But Mark didn't bob up. He wasn't bobbing at all.

So Jessame jumped in. She went right down to the bottom. She opened her eyes under the water and she grabbed hold of Mark's swimming trunks. Then with one hand and two feet she swam back up to the surface!

And there was her mum and lots of other people leaning over the edge of the pool. Some pulled Mark out of the water

and some pulled Jessame, and seconds later they were both on the grass-like side. Somebody was pressing Mark's chest and water was spouting out of his mouth.

Everyone was very quiet.

Then Mark sat up!

And people clapped.

Then people cheered.

Someone put a towel round Jessame's shoulders.

Vicki and Penny said, 'That was really brave, Jessame. You're a heroine.'

Later, when they were all having tea in Holly Bush House, Mum told everyone how she'd turned her back for just one moment and Mark had vanished.

Grandpa said, 'You did something very, very brave today, Jessame Aduke.'

And Jessame said, 'Yes Grandpa, I plunged. I really plunged. I hope someone will tell Mrs Crunkle.'

Grandpa said, 'Won't you tell her yourself, Jessame Aduke? Or better still show her?'

So Jessame thought about it and, while she was thinking, Mark came round to Jessame's chair. He opened his mouth wide and said, 'I'm Mark the Shark.' And she thought he was going to bite her, but he reached up and gave her a big slobbery kiss.

6

Jessame and the Ashobee

Jessame had lots of cousins and she liked nearly all of them, but she didn't like Cousin Iwanna.

Cousin Iwanna's real name was Iona. Mum and Grandma and Grandpa said that's what Jessame should call her, so Jessame did when she *said* her name, but when she *thought* about her it was Iwanna. Iwanna suited her because she said, 'I wanna! I wanna!' all the time – and she got! So Jessame sometimes called her Igotta! Iwanna got because Aunt Flo, who was her mother said, 'Yes, my poppet,' whenever Iwanna said, 'I wanna!'

And Aunt Flo said Jessame was spoiled! She did. Jessame had heard her. She'd said it to Jessame's mum. 'That girl is spoiled.' Just because Jessame had some new roller-skates.

But Iwanna had new things all the time. She had designer trainers and designer T-shirts, a computer and a bike, *and* she'd been a bridesmaid twice. Jessame had never been a bridesmaid.

It wasn't fair.

So Jessame didn't like Iwanna and she didn't like Aunt Flo either.

When they called at Holly Bush House one Friday evening Jessame pretended to be asleep. It was only half-pretending because she was nearly asleep on the small sofa, but if it had been someone nice she would have made herself wake up. Jessame could hear Aunt Flo's voice. So she closed her eyes again.

'We were just passing, so we thought we'd call and see how you were,' said Aunt Flo.

'How very kind,' said Grandpa.

'I'll put the kettle on,' said Grandma.

'I think there are some biscuits in the barrel,' said Jessame's mum.

'Roll out the barrel,' said Jacko. 'Let's have a barrel of laughs.'

But Jessame didn't feel like laughing or eating biscuits.

She felt like going to sleep.

Then someone poked her. 'I wanna tell you something, Jessame.'

Jessame kept very still.

'I wanna tell Jessame something!' Iwanna was shouting.

'Don't poke Jessame, Iona. Come and tell me,' said Grandpa.

Aunt Flo cackled. She poked Jessame. 'Iona has got something exciting to tell you, Jessame. Something very exciting.'

What could it be? More new trainers? More new dresses? Or a computer game?

Grandpa said, 'Jessame Aduke is very tired, Flo. I'll carry her to her bed, I think. We can tell her your news in the morning.'

Grandpa lifted Jessame and carried her

to bed.

'Night night, sleep tight, Jessame Aduke,' said Grandpa as he gently put her down and pulled the covers over her.

'Wake up in the morning bright.'

'To do what's right with all your might, Jessame,' said Grandma, kissing her cheek as she always did.

It was so nice being put to bed by Grandma and Grandpa, and it would have been perfect if Iwanna hadn't spoiled it.

She came in a few minutes later. Jessame didn't hear her because she was really asleep. But suddenly she was awake – wide awake, though still snuggled down and facing the wall – and Iwanna was saying, 'I'm going to be a bridesmaid, Jessame. And you're not. I'm going to be a bridesmaid to Auntie Carol.'

A bridesmaid! Again! That made three times! To Auntie Carol! Who *was* Auntie Carol?

All these thoughts went through

Jessame's head, but she didn't say anything. She closed her eyes and tried not to cry, because it was silly to cry about not being a bridesmaid.

In the morning, when Aunt Gbee came round, Jessame found out who Auntie Carol was. Uncle Gordon, who was Aunt Gbee's nephew-in-law, was getting married to someone called Carol, whom he'd met in the queue at Sainsbury's.

Aunt Gbee was Jessame's favourite aunt. There was only one thing wrong with Aunt Gbee as far as Jessame was concerned: she hadn't found Mr Right yet. Aunt Gbee said that, when she found Mr Right, Jessame could be her bridesmaid. But when would that be?

'It's no good moping, Jessame,' said Aunt Gbee. 'Carol would let you be a bridesmaid if you asked her, but you'd have to walk with Iona.'

Jessame thought about it. Did she really want to be a bridesmaid with Iwanna?

'Or,' said Aunt Gbee, looking Jessame up and down, 'you could be in the Ashobee. I think you're big enough now.'

Jessame thought Aunt Gbee had sneezed.

'In the what?'

The Ashobee wasn't a sneeze. It was the name given to special guests who all wore matching Ashobee dresses. 'They dance in them at the wedding,' Aunt Gbee explained.

'Dance?' said Jessame. 'In beautiful dresses?' Jessame loved dancing.

'Yes,' said Aunt Gbee.

'And I could be in it?' said Jessame.

'Yes,' said Aunt Gbee.

'Who said so?' Jessame could hardly believe it.

'*I* said so,' said Aunt Gbee, 'and I'm in charge of our Ashobee!'

There were two Ashobees. The bride's closest lady relations wore the Ashobee and so did the groom's. Aunt Gbee was in charge of Cousin Gordon's Ashobee, so she was going to market to choose some really lovely material. Jessame's mum was going to make the Ashobee.

'Can I help choose the really lovely material?' said Jessame.

'Yes,' said Aunt Gbee. 'You'll look as pretty as a paw paw flower.'

There was ever such a lot to do. First they had to go to Shepherd's Bush Market to look for materials. Then they had to have a meeting so that the ladies in the Ashobee could choose one of the patterns and the styles. Finally, Jessame's mum had to make them all.

On the very next Saturday, Jessame

went with her mum and Aunt Gbee to choose the material. Shepherd's Bush Market is a huge open air market with hundreds of stalls, and thousands of rolls of material.

Jessame had never seen so many colours and so many patterns. She thought she'd never be able to choose, but then she saw some red material – it was like poppy petals – with a golden thread running through it. That was it!

Aunt Gbee chose some black and white striped material and Jessame's Mum chose a shining yellow. It was a lovely yellow like the sun on a summer's day – but Jessame hoped and hoped the ladies of the Ashobee would choose the poppy red.

The stall holder gave them one metre of each material to take home and they all went back to Aunt Gbee's house in

Mare Street.

Aunt Molly, Aunt Sarah and Aunt Flo came round – without Cousin Iwanna. Everyone thought the poppy-red with the golden thread would be perfect. They all chose their styles, then Aunt Gbee went back to the market to buy one hundred metres of the lovely material.

Mum made Jessame's Ashobee first so that she could practise wearing it.

There were three pieces: a *gara*, which is a long wrapround skirt, a *lapa*, which is a short top and a head tie, which is a band of the same material tied round and round the head.

Jessame loved her Ashobee. It made her feel beautiful!

On the day of the wedding, Jessame didn't mind watching Iwanna walk up the aisle of St Bede's church behind Aunt Carol. And, at the reception in the

Bridge Hotel, she loved sitting with the ladies of the Ashobee at the top table behind the wedding cake.

After the feast, Uncle Sharp played a tune on his saxophone. Then the band struck up and the ladies of the Ashobee got to their feet. First they danced in a line – like a wave in the sea – swaying to and fro, to and fro to the music. Then they danced in a circle – with Jessame in the middle!

The wedding guests stood round them, clapping to the music. The dancing got faster and faster. And the clapping got louder and louder.

Jessame could feel the music and the clapping – and she danced in her red and gold Ashobee as she had never danced before.

She was a poppy dancing in a field.

She was a flame in a fire.

She was – JESSAME!
And she didn't want to be anyone else.